This is a work of fiction. Names, characters, places, and incidents either are the product of the author's imagination or are used fictitiously. Any resemblance to living or dead persons, events, business, companies, or locales is entirely coincidental.

Lost Miracle: Blood in the Water

Copyright © 2018 All rights reserved.

A Dragon Philosopher book.

Published through Kindle Direct Publishing.

www.dragonphilosopher.com

ISBN: 978-1-7328874-1-1

First addition Dec. 2018

Special thanks to my proof reader and editors B. Z. Smith, and Sherrie Olson. Couldn't have done any of this without them.

Cover produced by Dragon Philosopher team.

DRAGON PHILOSOPHER
TALES TO BE TOLD
www.dragonphilosopher.com

Books by Ann Riley

Vital Era

Lost Miracle Blood in the Water

Tied Souls (Jan. 2019)

Lost Miracle

Blood in the Water

Ann Riley

Chapter 1

Atlantic Ocean, May 16, 2106
- 12:36 p.m.

The day was full of movement as the ocean played

about. Waves pushed along, while seagulls danced across

the surface. Clouds floated high above, watching and

waiting for a chance to cause chaos. A breeze blew

across the water, lifting the birds and waves alike, giving

them energy.

The view from a lonely ship was nothing but

water; the black ship floated peacefully. The vessel had

recently been in the Labrador Sea and was coming into

the Atlantic Ocean. It looked similar to a cargo ship from

a hundred years ago but was half the size. There was one huge cube-shaped container on deck. It had a gray exterior and could only be moved by a crane. The ship's crane was located amidships, with a speedboat next to it, and a railing around the ship's deck.

The bridge tower was built into the stern of the ship. It had several long antennas on the roof, with windows outlining the top. Black walls covered the tower with two doors at its base. One on the starboard side, and the other on the port side.

Lost Miracle was painted in white on the bow of the ship. The paint was worn from years on the ocean.

Lost Miracle shared a secret with four other ships. This shared secret was one of corruption within the U.S. government. Though there had been corruption since the time of the founding fathers, this was something more intense. The government was a charade of its former ways.

The crew of the peaceful ship was about to receive news. The news was going to change the course they had started on.

Captain's Quarters - 12:38 p.m.

The captain's quarters was a small cabin in the ship; it had a small bed with a shelf at its head, a small desk with a cupboard, a rolling chair, and a table. Three people sat around the table, with papers scattered all about. The crew members had gone over all the documents and couldn't believe the information.

The older man of the trio wore a captain's uniform with dark gray pants and a matching jacket, and a white collared shirt underneath. He was bald with dark tan skin. He had a few wrinkles on his forehead.

Andres Swann was his name, and he was Captain of Lost Miracle for the past ten years.

The woman next to him wore a button-up shirt with a skirt, and her braided gray hair looked charming against her olive complexion.

Her name was Madeline Crowe; she kept the ship's crew together.

The last man had thick brown hair and pale skin. He wore a white lab coat over his clothes for his duties as the doctor. He was a little younger than the other two. Doctor was his title, and Koby Bailey was his name.

The three of them had carefully read the papers on the table. The documents had been transmitted that morning; the information was on the death of the former President of the United States, Ian Young. The significance was Ian Young, ten years ago, had organized the mission, that Lost Miracle and the four other ships were part of. The mission was his last act as Commander and Chief, but with his sudden death it had become uncertain.

"What do you think they will do with the body?" Koby asked.

Crowe frowned, "Bergen will probably order for him to be thrown into the ocean, to show how traitors are treated. She is the one who forced his impeachment."

"Really?" Koby's face was covered in shock.

Captain Swann shook his head, "they'll keep the body until the investigation into Young's crimes has been completed."

The shock faded from Koby's face.

Crowe picked up a paper, "the question I have, is who this hero is that killed Young? I thought the government was done with super-powered people after the Oregon's tragedy? That the nation was no longer going to promote heroes to the public because they weren't controllable."

"Ghost shadow is his name, was he part of those same heroes?" Koby wondered, "I don't remember all their names."

"No, he wasn't there ten years ago," Crowe informed, "he's new."

"So we'll have nothing on him," Koby sighed.

"Well, we did get data. He isn't tech-powered like the Oregon heroes; his powers are supernatural," she put the paper back on the table, "and more or less he's an enforcer for the government."

"Oh, the name Ghost Shadow wasn't random then," Koby rubbed the back of his neck, "I wonder what his ability is? Maybe shadows or telekinesis; I hope it's not mind reading."

"Either way," Crowe looked at Koby, "we're the villain, and he's the hero."

"We need to tell the twins," Captain Swann changed the topic.

The other two looked at the Captain in uncertainty.

"And who should do that?" Crowe inquired.

Koby frowned, "I don't want to tell them that their father was murdered."

"Aren't doctors suppose to be compassionate and caring," Captain Swann pointed out.

Koby shook his head, "sorry Captain, but I don't want to deliver the bad news. Tegan was in charge of communications for the White House when we worked for the government and is still in charge of them now; she should do it."

"Stop worrying Doc," Crowe sighed, "they probably already know."

"Really?" Captain Swann stood up, "we just barely found out."

Crowe stood up too, "they are notorious for sneaking around, and spying on others."

"True," Captain Swann paused before switching subjects again, "after we make sure the twins know; we need to find out where Young's body will be."

Koby scratched his chin, "that will be hard, it's not like a dead man's whereabouts are announced."

Koby stood up too, and the three adults left the room.

Main Deck – 12:40 p.m.

A teenage boy leaned against the huge gray container on deck opposite the crane and speedboat; he held copies of the documents the adults had been reading.

The Boy's name was Terry Young. He wore a button-up shirt with a black vest and matching dress pants. His black hair was slicked back and shined in the sunlight.

"Well," Terry sighed, "this is one way to find out your father's been murdered."

He looked up from the papers towards his sister. She stood across from him, leaning against the railing.

Mary Young was her name; she gazed up at the sky. Her black hair was pulled back, and it seemed to be the only thing she shared with her brother. She dressed drastically different, with a plain t-shirt, jeans, and a jacket.

"I'm not shocked," Terry frowned, "father didn't know what safety was, even when the secret service was there. Probably from his days in the military."

She continued to gaze upward, "what should we do?"

"Give up," he stated, "we never knew who he was fighting, and we could make a good life. And make our own decisions."

Mary looked at her brother and frowned, "you didn't read the last page."

Terry wrinkled his forehead and looked at the documents again. After several seconds of reading, he let another sigh out.

"The hero who killed Ian Young, who the government is supporting, is personally tracking down the Young family, for it is believed they aided and abetted him," Terry read aloud.

He looked up at his sister and sighed once again, "rats, I hate heroes."

Radio Room - 1:06 p.m.

The last of the crew was in the radio room. The room had two port windows, a table in the middle, and a line of counters to one side with radio base stations on them. Each radio had dials, headsets, and chairs in front. The stations looked like old ones from a hundred years ago, but they were secured and high-powered, nothing could hack them.

Three people worked in the room. Two of them were at the radio stations, while the other stood by the table. The woman at the table was going through new documents that had been transmitted.

Chloe Holt was the woman's name. She managed the ship's security. Her clothes were a collared shirt and neutral dress pants. The blond hair on her head was pulled into a bun, and she looked like she had been tanning on a beach.

"Young stole data from the F.B.I. before they killed him," Chloe read, "they haven't located it. So we'll need to get the data before they find it."

"Does it say what the data is?" the man sitting at a radio station asked.

He wore dirty overalls because he was the engineer for the ship. His name was Reece Shaw.

"There's no info on the data," Chloe answered. "Have you contacted the other ships, Tegan?"

The other woman at a different station was listening with one ear in a headset, "yes, except Hallowed."

Her name, Tegan Bruce, was on her chef's jacket. Her duties were cooking and communications.

"The rest have received the news and are waiting for our answer on whether we're going to continue the mission," Tegan ran a hand through her light red hair.

"Okay, I'll inform the Captain," Chloe walked to the end station.

She flipped several switches, "doesn't seem to be anyone in the bridge, I'm going to find him."

Chloe left the room.

Navigation Room – 1:34 p.m.

Chloe walked briskly down the metal passageway Swann hadn't been in the captain's quarters. She was now heading towards the navigation room. If he weren't there, she would have to start over.

Walking up to the metal door, Chloe entered the room. The navigation room was well lit, by a large table that filled the area. The table displayed a digital map of the world. Five tiny virtual ships could be seen on it, with their coordinates being shown next to them. Only one of the ships hadn't been updated for the last few months.

Captain Swann was standing at the table looking at the map; his gaze shifted to Chloe, "coming with news?"

Chloe nodded, "all of our ships have received the news and are awaiting our response."

Swann rubbed his bald head, "did Hallowed respond?"

She shook her head.

He nodded.

"Sir," Chloe handed him papers from the radio room, "is the data Young got worth trying to get?"

Captain Swann sighed, "yes."

"You realize we aren't in America anymore?" she stated, "you don't have your job as chief of staff for President Young. You don't have to worry about Young's interests. We could try living somewhere else."

Captain Swann's face remained neutral, "when did his interests stop mattering? Or when did we stop caring?"

She couldn't answer him.

"Chloe," Captain Swann rubbed his head again, "I understand that you, like everyone on the ships, and are tired of fighting. But we aren't fighting because one man told us too. We are fighting because it's not over. Young was the first to die in over ten years, but he probably isn't the last. I may not be the chief of staff anymore, but that doesn't change the situation."

The room was silent for a few moments.

"So what's next?" Chloe inquired.

"Changing of course," Captain Swann frowned at the map.

Chloe gave the map a tired look.

Chapter 2
Radio Room, May 19, 2106
– 9:56 a.m.

Tegan sat in the radio room. She had a new chef jacket on, and her red hair pulled back into a ponytail. Sunlight illuminated the room, letting natural light fill the area.

She had a headset on, as she worked at one of the radio stations. She twisted a dial and listened intensely. A signal had been sent by one of the other ships, and she was trying to contact them. Static was all that was coming through, and it was highly annoying.

"Come on," she muttered.

Flipping a switch, the static on the station became recognizable.

"Lost Miracle, this is Bala, come in," a voice said.

"Yes," Tegan looked for a microphone, but none were out, and the stations needed one because of their design like old tech.

She scrambled to a drawer. Opening it, she grabbed a microphone from within. She brought the microphone out quickly, not realizing the cord was caught, pulling on it caused the cabinet to lean until it gave way to gravity. The drawer crashed to the floor, echoing throughout the ship.

Tegan flinched, "crap."

She untangled the cord from the drawer, before going back to her station. She plugged the microphone in, like the olden days.

"Lost Miracle responding, do you hear me, Bala, over?" she spoke into the microphone.

"We hear you," the voice answered, "we have received news on Ian Young's body, over."

"Standby," Tegan grabbed a pen and paper, "ready for the info."

"An F.B.I. informant told us that they will be holding custody for Young. They have to keep the body in a morgue near an F.B.I. Station," the voice informed, "so they don't draw suspicion."

"They couldn't give us a location?" she inquired.

"No, but the info should be accessible from any F.B.I. location," the voice answered.

"Thank you, out" she turned the radio off.

She looked at the notes. Chloe entered the room, and Tegan turned to her.

"I got a message on my phone that a ship was trying to contact us by radio," Chloe said, "what did the ships have for us?"

"Info on who has Young's body. Do you think you can take this to the Captain?" Tegan asked Chloe, "It's from Bala."

She looked at the papers Tegan handed her, "sure."

Captain's Quarters — 10:11 a.m.

Chloe walked up to the Captain's door and knocked. The sound echoed through the ship.

"Come in," Captain Swann called from inside.

She entered the room. Swann sat at the table; he wore a different gray captain's uniform with his bald head reflecting the light. He was reading documents about weather conditions but looked up as Chloe walked in. She sat down next to him.

"Did Tegan make contact?" Swann asked.

"Yes, the F.B.I. is holding Young's body," she informed.

He nodded slowly, "I would have thought C.I.A. I guess they're trying to make it easy. Hopefully, it doesn't get noticed by Bergen."

"But we don't know the location," Chloe stated, "we'll have to hack an F.B.I. server."

She paused, she was uneasy with the information.

Captain Swann gave her a funny look, "and?"

Chloe sighed, "we won't be able to hack unless we're in an F.B.I. Station. Their security won't let any access happen from the outside; it's too hard to try and get through their firewall."

"I remember when they installed that during President Young's administration. It will help with appearances for Bergen so she won't suspect the informant," he nodded again, "okay, we need to go to the nearest port with a location."

Captain Swann started going through the documents on the table until he found the right one. He skimmed the paper. It had a list of ports along the east coast, with little bits of info about them.

"We will be going to Zolis Port," he announced, "it's the nearest station that is big enough to have access to federal files in the Bureau. Which means we'll be going to Maine."

Swann rubbed his head as he started thinking of a plan.

Mess Hall — 11:41 a.m.

The mess hall was slightly bigger than the radio room. There were three round tables with chairs around them. Two doors, one to the galley, or the kitchen as the twins called it, and one to a passageway.

Terry sat at one of the tables; he had a sucker in his mouth. His sister sat next to him; she had her head on the table with her eyes closed. The two of them looked like they were still wearing the same clothes from the other day.

Crowe walked into the mess hall from the passageway; her eyes landed on the twins, as she walked over to them and sat down next to Mary.

"I've been looking for the two of you," she stated.

Mary sat up and opened her eyes, "we've been here for the last hour."

Crowe sighed.

"I like your skirt," Terry commented, smirking, "is it new?"

"Don't distract me," she warned, "we need to talk about the new mission."

Mary frowned, "I thought we were giving up?"

"No," Crowe said sternly, "we're going to pick up the fight from where your father left it."

"How?" Terry looked confused, "he kept everything to himself."

"We may not know what he had," she explained, "but your father's body will have the data."

"How can his body have data?" Mary asked.

"His teeth," Crowe informed, "a tooth of his is data storage."

"But why are you talking to us about it?" Terry finished his sucker, he stood up and walked over to a garbage can throwing it away.

"We're going to need your skills to retrieve the data, and locate his body," Crowe explained.

The twins gave her a funny look.

"Skills?" Terry didn't understand; he put his hands on his hips.

"The skills your father had you develop," she pointed out.

"Oh," Mary and Terry both said, they shared a look across the room.

"Our computer skills," Mary clarified.

Crowe nodded.

Bridge – 12:22 p.m.

The bridge was the brain of the ship. The steering, throttle, and intercom systems were there. It also had the best view being at the top of the tower, with windows facing the bow of the ship. This is where decisions could be made.

Captain Swann climbed the ladder, the twins called them stairs, on the outside of the tower. He entered the bridge. The ship's controls were there waiting to be used on panels. The ship had an automatic system that worked like autopilot so that a skeleton crew could run the system. The modifications were the only reason a crew of fewer than ten people could man the ship.

He walked to a panel with the intercom system controls. Swann turned the system on. Squeaks erupted from the speakers throughout the ship before going silent. The metal echoed all the noises, making it sound like an army of mice.

"Good afternoon," Captain Swann spoke into the system, "with the changing of our mission, comes a changing of course. We will be going to Zolis port in Maine, to break into and hack an F.B.I. Station. Be prepared for these actions. Upon charting our course, I will need Reece and Tegan to meet me in the navigation room around one o'clock."

Swann flipped a switch, and power to the intercom system turned off, with a squeak of protest. The ears of the Captain and crew ached from the system's use.

Navigation Room – 1:07 p.m.

The map illuminated the navigation room, casting weak light on the faces looking at it. Captain Swann and Tegan were the only ones in the room. Tegan still had her chef's jacket on, with a new red smudge on the front. She had tried to wash the stain away but hadn't succeeded yet. Three of the little ships had moved on the map, while

Hallowed remained still. The virtual Lost Miracle ship on the map was the only one that moved steadily, it was connected to the ship.

"So this might be the last time we can go to port without being criminals for a while," Swann pointed to the port so Tegan could see it, "we need to stock up. We won't be making stops unless it's an emergency."

She leaned in closer, "we can do that…why isn't Reece here?"

Tegan looked at him.

"Engine trouble," he explained, "I'll be going over the course with him at another time."

She straightened her stance, "before we go breaking laws, we'll need a few days to collect supplies, at least I'll need a day or two…also you should tell Koby, just in case he needs supplies for the doctor's office. I know we have to hurry, but we're going to need time to prepare for this voyage of crime we're about to take."

He nodded slowly, "good advice. I will inform Koby, and I will take into account about waiting to break the law."

Swann and Tegan left, leaving the map to illuminate an empty room.

Chapter 3
Bridge, May 23, 2106 — 7:26 a.m.

Early sunlight filtered through the windows of the bridge, casting a glow on the control panels and throughout the room. Captain Swann and Chloe guided Lost Miracle closer to Zolis Port. They were too big to enter, so they stationed themselves just outside.

Chloe pulled her jacket tighter around herself; the morning chill wasn't bad, it just made sure you didn't forget about it. Captain Swann didn't notice the cold, other than having a baseball cap on. The ship continued to slow down, with small waves radiating from it through the ocean.

Swann didn't look away from the controls, "are you and the twins ready?"

"Yes," Chloe nodded, "we are ready to go tonight."

"That's good," Captain Swann continued to decrease the speed of the ship, "but Tegan and Reece need to go to shore so you won't be leaving for a couple of days."

Chloe made a face at Swann, "I understand we need supplies, but we could still do it tonight after a day of loading."

Swann shook his head, "we're going to become fugitives again, we need more than one day for prepping."

Chloe nodded again, "fine, I understand that, but staying near a port for too long is bad. Someone might recognize Lost Miracle. The easiest target is a non-moving one."

Captain Swann finally brought the ship to a full stop in the water, "I get your concern, but this risk can't be helped. We need to take it."

Radio Room, May 25, 2106 - 12:12 a.m.

Two days had gone by since Lost Miracle arrived at Zolis Port. The collecting of supplies had been completed, and the mission to break into a federal building had started.

Only ceiling lights illuminated the radio room; the port windows showed darkness outside. Reece sat at one of the stations. He had changed out of his overalls and was wearing a plain t-shirt and jeans. He had a headset on and was listening to Zolis radio stations.

Tegan walked into the room holding a box of crackers. Her chef jacket was unbuttoned, which allowed her to relax as she sat next to Reece. She placed the crackers in front of him.

"Thanks," Reece smiled at Tegan.

"No problem," Tegan stretched, "any alerts?"

"Nope, there hasn't been any disturbances in the city," Reece opened the box, "did you get all the supplies needed?"

Tegan rubbed her face, "yeah, and even the stuff Koby needed. I don't get why he couldn't get it himself."

"Because the last time he was on American soil, he lost his job as secretary of Health and Human Services, while having his face plastered on all the news circuits as a terrorist for killing the vice president," Reece reminded her.

The room went silent. Reece continued to listen to the radio, as Tegan thought to herself.

"So they aren't going to the port?" Tegan gazed at Reece, changing the subject.

"Right," he looked back at her, "they're going to the shoreline a couple of miles away from the port so they won't be noticed."

"And that's because of us?" Tegan asked.

"Somewhat," Reece shrugged, "Captain thinks it would cause more attention if they showed up in the same boat we used for supplies."

Tegan nodded slowly, "Okay, I guess I get it."

Zolis Port -12:38 a.m.

Terry, Mary, and Chloe were in the speedboat. They all wore jackets to protect themselves from the chill and spray from the ocean. The black water made it feel like it was an invasion, giving the twins feelings of uncertainty but Chloe was unaffected. She steered the boat like it was an average day.

They could see the Zolis port as they continued through the water. It was an average size port, it couldn't fit large ships, but it supported many smaller boats. There were lights on for the graveyard shift. There weren't many advancements in technology, the port had been built in the 2020s, and hadn't changed since then.

Chloe steered the boat and headed to the shoreline about a mile away from the port. They were passing it at an angle. The people working there wouldn't be able to see them.

"You two ready?" Chloe asked she felt their uneasiness.

Mary held on to the bag she was carrying, "yeah."

Terry let a sigh out, "yes, we've been over the plan. I just want to get it over with because I'm sick of hearing about it. That's all that was talked about for these last two days. I would have killed for any other conversation."

"Don't worry," Chloe looked over her shoulder at them, "we'll get to the shore soon, then make our way to the station."

Mary watched her brother let out another sigh and stare at the port. She continued to hold onto her bag. She was the only one with gear, her laptop and other supplies were in the pack.

Lost Miracle, Main Deck

– 12:55 a.m.

Crowe and Koby walked together, parallel to the railing in the darkness. Crowe had a coat pulled over, while Koby pulled his white lab coat tighter around himself. They were coming from a hatch from the head of the ship that led to the crew's quarters. They could have reached the bridge by going within the ship, but it was quicker to go aft, or as the twins would say across the deck.

"We need Reece to be in the engine room if suddenly we need to flee or fight," Crowe informed, "so you'll go replace him in the radio room."

"But isn't Tegan there?" Koby struggled against the cold.

"She is, but having two in the room to help monitor is better," she explained, "we don't want to mess this up just because our radios got overwhelmed."

"Fine, but what if we need to use our defense system?" Koby inquired.

"Reece can handle the engine," Crowe explained, "he just has to be in there, so nothing goes wrong. We don't want to fry our system just for one shot against a port with no military."

"Okay," Koby nodded.

"I'll be going to the bridge to help with the Captain. We will keep in contact through the intercom system," Crowe walked up the ladder to the tower.

Koby opened one of the doors at the base and entered.

Bridge – 1:01 a.m.

Swann sat in a chair in the front of the controls waiting. He hadn't moved from the bridge since the speedboat had left. Crowe opened the door and entered the room. Captain Swann glanced at her as she walked over and sat down in a chair next to him. He had expected she would come.

"They'll be fine," Crowe comforted, saying it more for herself.

Swann sighed and rubbed his bald head, "I don't feel good about sending them, I know you don't either. But no one else has computer skills like them, and the other ships aren't in a position to do this. This was our only option."

"I know," Crowe leaned forward in her chair, "I wish they could have a safe life and not have to deal with this."

"We all wish that," Swann said.

"Yeah, I know," Crowe sighed again, "and I know you wish you could take their spot, so they wouldn't have to go break into a federal building in the middle of the night."

Captain Swann gave Crowe a sympathetic look, "they've got Chloe to protect them, and the whole crew watching out for them…some people only have one person who cares or no one."

Crowe gave him a sad smile, "well, they're not the only ones who shouldn't be doing this. I sometimes wonder where we would all be if we weren't stuck to Lost Miracle."

"Still in politics," Captain Swann smiled softly.

Crowe chuckled humorlessly, "glad I'm here."

Chapter 4

Zolis City, May 25, 2106 - 1:34 a.m.

Terry, Mary, and Chloe entered the quiet city from the west side, dark square buildings lined its streets.

Chloe held a device showing a digital map of Zolis, "we take a left here."

The trio turned a corner and continued to walk on the sidewalk down the street through the city. There weren't very many people out during the night.

"How much longer?" Mary asked, her nerves were tensed up from the unknown.

"Ten minutes," Chloe calculated.

Terry didn't mind being in a new place. He liked to explore. His eyes looked at the buildings they passed, as they continued down the street.

"We need to go right," Chloe informed, "we should almost be there."

"Good," Mary commented."

Terry gave his sister a funny look, "if Chloe had hijacked a car we could have gotten to the station faster."

Chloe sighed, "walking gives us a better layout of the city."

Terry snorted, "or gives us a better chance of being spotted."

The trio took another corner and walked down the street to the F.B.I. building. They stood in front of it. The building was square like the other structures around. It appeared to have four floors with a parking garage underneath. It wasn't special.

"How are we going to get in?" Mary inquired.

Chloe put her digital map away, "through the garage. I have a skeleton key card from when I worked in the Secret Service."

"And you kept it? That's unlike you." Terry pointed out.

"Going on the run requires many things," Chloe explained.

F.B.I. Station – 1:55 a.m.

Chloe opened a door from the F.B.I.'s garage into the building. She put the skeleton key card away and led her small team to a flight of stairs. Terry and Mary followed her up to the floor above. Mary had a phone out and was working on getting the security cameras in a loop. She had already hacked the garage and first two floors.

The inside of the station was generic for a federal building, with gray hallways and black tile. Chloe led them through a door and into a hall, they walked towards a corner. Terry and Mary crept behind her, feeling uncomfortable.

Chloe peeked around the corner and saw a camera. She drew herself back. Her instincts made her want to leave.

"Are you sure you took care of the security system?" she looked at the twins.

Terry gave Chloe an annoyed look, "the security guards don't see a thing."

Mary nodded, she put her phone away, "I sent a Trojan virus to cover are entrance. Then I took care of the cameras before they could register the loop."

"Okay," Chloe sighed and turned the corner, glancing at the camera before walking up to the door.

She took out lock pick tools, and worked on the lock; this door didn't have a keycard slot. Kneeling down revealed a gun strapped to her ankle.

"Hey," Terry pointed at it, "why don't we get a gun?"

Chloe continued to work on the lock, "it's a stun gun, and the reason you don't have one is that you fired one at the engine of our ship. Causing everything to lose power for twelve hours; we don't want something like that happening again."

Terry went silent. Mary patted her brother on the shoulder.

"They don't even let us have whistles anymore, so don't feel bad," Mary smiled at her brother, "we still get candy, so can't complain."

Chloe unlocked the door, and the three of them went deeper into the station, going across the black tile and down another gray hall into the unwelcoming place.

Offices – 2:08 a.m.

Terry walked into a section of the building full of cubicles; the square spaces looked like a maze in the dark. He took a seat, plugged in his flash drive, and turned the computer on. Mary opened her bag; she pulled out a small laptop. She connected it to the computer with a cable, after a few seconds of her typing Terry gained access and started searching through documents. Everything he worked on was filed into the flash drive.

"Thanks, Mary," Terry focused on the glowing screen.

Mary disconnected her laptop and placed it back into her bag. The three of them went silent, only the clicking from the keyboard filled the room. Chloe walked to a window and looked out into the night. Mary watched her brother work; the glow from the computer screen made the room feel darker.

A buzzing came from Chloe's phone; she took it out. A message was on the screen; from someone she hadn't seen in years. He knew she was there in Zolis, but hadn't realize where she was at that moment.

"I can't get the info from here," Terry conceited.

Chloe looked up from her phone, "how do we get it?"

"Locate to a higher ranking individual," Mary answered, "someone's computer that already has the access or we'll be here all night."

Terry started a new search for the closest computer with access to classified documents. The search didn't take long.

"We need to go up a floor," he informed, "and to an office under the name Haber."

"Okay," Chloe put her phone away and marched towards the stairwell. Her nerves were on high alert from the message on the phone.

Terry turned the computer off and followed after Chloe with his sister. They had to run to keep up with her marching.

Haber's Office - 2:18 a.m.

The trio walked onto the third floor after Chloe picked the lock of the stairwell door. Terry guided them to a specific office on the floor. They opened the door and went into the little office.

The desk in the middle was full of stuff; post-it notes, and pictures scattered about. Two windows in the office faced the entrance to the parking garage. Chloe walked up to the windows and looked out. Mary took her laptop out again and plugged it in. Terry sat in front of the computer, waiting. He watched the black screen patiently.

"This guy likes dogs," Terry commented.

"At least he has something," Mary whispered, "the computer should be running now. It's all yours."

Terry plugged his flash drive in and went to work, as the screen came alive. Mary unhooked her laptop and put it away for the second time that night. She stayed by the desk.

"I have a location on my father's body," Terry announced.

"That's fast," Mary pointed out.

"Someone else has been looking at the data recently," Terry explained, "a man name Pearson, he accessed it last night, around this time."

Chloe flinched at the name, but the twins didn't notice her reaction, "Terry see if you can get any data on the hero, like what his abilities are. I want to know what his power could be."

Terry typed the hero's name into the computer, "It's a good thing heroes are government employees, the F.B.I. should have all the data we need."

Headlights from a car flashed in the windows, as a vehicle pulled into the F.B.I.'s parking garage. Chloe ducked down along with Mary; Terry didn't notice as his attention was on the computer. Fear started to rise in Mary, as she crawled towards the door. Chloe peaked out the window, but the vehicle was already gone.

Lost Miracle, Radio Room

- 2:25 a.m.

It was way past midnight, and the radio room was full of activity. Tegan worked at one of the radio stations, her chef jacket off. Koby, his white lab coat still on, sat at the table behind her looking through several documents, these papers had past information for their small group of ships. They outlined the protocol for communication.

The duo had been working at the stations for the last few hours. A signal had been sent, and they couldn't find it again. Koby was almost ready to call the bridge for help.

"Have you tried all the stations?" Koby continued to scan the documents.

"Yes, I've gone through all the ones we use," Tegan shook her head in frustration, "Gold Rose isn't on any of them."

51

"They sent the code the right way," Koby sighed, "but now we can't seem to find them on any of the stations. Even the backup stations. What's the point of having a security code over the radio, if it just backfires? This is ridiculous! It doesn't have to be this difficult, even if we are using antique radios."

Tegan adjusted one of the dials, "have you found any stations in the papers? Any at all?"

Koby picked up a paper, looking at it. Making sure his mind wasn't misremembering what he had read.

Koby sighed again, "yes…have you tried the old station, from before we started working against the government? The first one we used when the ships were close together."

"Trying it now," Tegan flipped a switch.

"Lost Miracle, please come in!" a voice yelled over the station.

The loud voice made Koby and Tegan jump.

"Gold Rose, this is Lost Miracle," Tegan responded into a microphone.

"Finally, we've been trying to contact you for over twenty hours now," the voice stated.

"Really?" Koby gave Tegan a confused look, "we just barely got the code for contact an hour ago."

Tegan ignored Koby, "why the urgency?"

"Your ship has been tagged," the voice informed, "the hero has entered the city to investigate Lost Miracle under his handler's name, Pearson. I'm sorry we didn't catch it earlier."

Tegan turned to Koby, "contact Chloe."

Koby grabbed his phone from the table and dialed.

"Thank you, Gold Rose, out," Tegan switched the radio.

She turned to the intercom controls and turned them on. Squeaks erupted throughout the metal beast.

Chapter 5

Haber's Office, May 25, 2106

- 2:39 a.m.

The trio hadn't moved from Haber's office. Chloe crouched by the window, while Mary sat at the door listening for any movement. Terry still sat at the computer typing. Searching through the documents wasn't going as fast as expected.

"Well," Terry sighed, "there doesn't seem to be too much on Ghost Shadow. There isn't even a billing address, which is unheard of. The only thing that stands out is he came from a place where human experimentation happened, probably where he got his

55

powers. But he does have a handler, who supervises him while he's working for the government, that came from Washington, let me see if I can get his name."

Mary gave her brother a confused look, "handler?"

"I would guess it's like a sidekick," Terry suggested, "don't heroes usually have sidekicks?"

Buzzing from Chloe's pocket caught her attention again. Chloe pulled out the phone and answered it, "yeah?"

"Someone just logged in," Terry announced, "they're on the second floor."

"That's not good to hear," Mary's face covered in fright.

"We need to go now," Chloe still had the phone next to her ear, "we just received data that the hero is in Zolis. And the man you saw looking up the location of

Young's body from the second floor, Pearson, is his handler."

Terry flinched at the news, "that's definitely not good."

"Why?" Mary asked.

"The sidekick just logged into a computer downstairs," Terry explained, "probably here with the hero."

"Lost Miracle," Chloe spoke into the phone, "we're about to be discovered prepare for action. We will be crossing paths with Ghost Shadow."

Mary clutched her bag tighter. Terry grabbed his flash drive and handed it to Mary, who put it away in her bag. Chloe hung up the phone.

F.B.I. Station– 2:49 a.m.

Chloe led the twins out of Haber's office. She hurried to the stairwell and opened the door. Terry and Mary rushed down the stairs quickly. They didn't look behind themselves until the bottom floor, Chloe hadn't followed.

"Where's Chloe?" Terry whispered.

Mary turned to her brother, "I don't know."

"Who are you? And why are you making so much noise at this hour?" the questions rang out from the stairs platform between the first floor and parking lot.

Terry and Mary looked up. An average height man stood on the platform. His tan complexion looked light because of his shaven head and oversized black coat. Something felt off about the man, something was unreal.

Mary backed away.

Terry placed himself closer to the door, "we're I.T.?"

"Wait," the man leaned closer, "I've seen your faces."

"Oh no," Mary whispered.

"The photo wasn't good," black tentacles started rising from the man's pockets in his jacket, they shimmered in the light, "but there's no mistake, your Ian Young's children."

"He's the hero," Terry shook with fear at seeing the tentacles rise.

The hero readied his three black tentacles, they prepared to strike downward. The sound of electricity stopped the hero. He fell from the platform and down the stairs, with the tentacles losing their density and turning into a liquid, splashing onto the stairs. Chloe stood where the man had been, her stun gun in hand.

Before Chloe could say anything, a man watching from the stairs above, tackled her. The two adults wrestled on the platform between the first floor and parking lot. The man was taller and had a plain t-shirt with cargo pants on. His short black hair was unaffected by the wrestling, but his dark tan skin was going to have bruises.

"What should we do?" Mary asked.

Terry looked at the unconscious hero on the stairs, "we could try to help."

Chloe pushed the man off, but he grabbed onto her, causing them to tumble down the rest of the stairs, landing on the hero, and hitting their heads on each other, they roll down the stairs, between the twins, and bang into the door at the bottom. Breaking the door's handle and opening it.

The taller man, the hero and Chloe laid on the ground next to each other with the twins looking at them.

The taller man was now unconscious like the hero, and Chloe was bloody from a few scratches.

"You okay?" Mary walked over to Chloe

"Well," Terry helped her stand up, "they say never meet your heroes."

Chloe sighed at Terry's comment. The twins started running towards the exit, while Chloe bent down and took the handler's watch from his wrist.

Streets of Zolis - 3:15 a.m.

Terry drove a car Chloe had hijacked through roads illuminated with streetlights. Mary was sitting in back putting bandages on Chloe's cuts. She had gotten the bandages from her first aid kit in her bag, and had taken care of Chloe's left arm and was working on her face. Chloe looked out the back window; she had her phone to her ear as she tried to contact Lost Miracle.

"Koby!" Chloe yelled into the phone, "we're being pursued...no not a shot from the defense system, just cause waves to disrupt the dock."

Chloe ended the conversation and put the phone away. Terry looked in the rearview mirror and saw headlights speeding towards them. He accelerated their vehicle. Mary and Chloe viewed the lights coming.

"What should we do?" Mary asked.

"Terry," Chloe rolled down a back window, "keep driving towards the speedboat."

Terry nodded, focusing on the road. He didn't let the other vehicle distract him from driving.

"Do you think it's the hero?" Mary asked.

"The stun gun will keep the hero unconscious for hours, but," Chloe stuck her head out of the window, "definitely didn't knock the handler out good."

She took her stun gun from her belt and aimed it at the vehicle. It didn't look like it could do much.

"Is that even going to reach him?" Mary looked at the headlights worried.

Chloe fired the gun. It sent a yellow beam towards the other vehicle, the sound of electricity followed the light. It struck its mark. The power in the car surged, before turning off and stopping. Terry drove them away from the scene.

Zolis Port – 3:19 a.m.

The Zolis port was calm as the graveyard shift continued. There wasn't anything unusual going on, as the workers continued working. It was a chilly night, but the people there were used to the weather. To them, it was a pleasant night.

The black ship, Lost Miracle, was heading for the port at an angle. The ship was going at an accelerated pace, and it was coming unseen. Daylight would have allowed warning signals to be given, but the darkness concealed the metal beast.

Lost Miracle cruised by the port with big waves following behind. The workers cried out in surprise as the waves went through the port. They crashed against sea vessels and the dock. They made it unstable and rocked every boat, causing some vessels to sway violently against the wooden planks. Panic surged, with workers trying to keep the boats safe from being lost.

The waves made it impossible for any boat to go through the water, or for anyone to track the black ship cruising away. Some people saw the metal beast, but the chaos all around consumed their attention. It would be several minutes before anyone could go out to deep water. There was a great fear of capsizing with the waves going wild.

Lost Miracle was free from harassment, but the group on land still had their pursuers coming after them, they just wouldn't be gaining any new ones from the port anymore.

Speedboat - 3:27 a.m.

Terry drove the car onto the beach, and into a hole. The front tires kicked sand up, as the passengers realized it wasn't going anywhere. Their plans changed again.

"Run," Chloe opened the car door and jumped out.

Terry and Mary followed, running right behind her. They sprinted across the sand, leaving footprints. The trio made it to the speedboat. Mary threw her bag in and helped push the boat back into the water with the others. The three of them managed to get the speedboat into the ocean and jumped aboard. The waves at the port didn't cause them any trouble, they were too far away.

A truck drove past their abandoned vehicle, and up to where the boat had been. It stopped, shining its headlights on the speedboat drifting away from the shoreline. Pearson, the tall man, got out and stared at them. Chloe locked eyes with him.

"Good thing the hero isn't here," Mary whispered.

Chloe broke eye contact with the handler, and took control of the steering; she directed them out to the open ocean. The twins continued to watch the handler as he shrunk from their sight. There was no way for him to continue the chase.

"One of you needs to call Lost Miracle, so we know where to go," Chloe informed, she took her phone out of her pocket.

Terry took Chloe's phone and started to dial for Lost Miracle. Mary continued to watch the coast, as she clutched her bag.

"What do you think the black tentacles were?"

Mary whispered, "could they be poisonous?"

No one could answer.

Chapter 6

Bridge, May 27, 2106

- 12:56 p.m.

Warm sunlight splashed into the bridge. Captain Swann was in the room with Reece. Swann sat down, loosening his shirt's collar. Reece held papers while sitting next to Swann. His overalls had recently been cleaned, so he smelled like soap.

"What's the problem?" Swann asked.

Reece sighed, "the engine seems to have a hiccup, the power system has a glitch, and the defense system is stiff. Maintenance will be needed."

Captain Swann nodded slowly, "the old torpedo tubes still operational?"

"Yes," Reece answered, "those have shown no signs of a problem, and are probably the most reliable thing right now."

"What about the intercom system?" Captain Swann glanced at its controls, "that system hurts everyone ears when used. It's almost not worth having."

Reece shrugged, "I don't know what to tell you, Captain. That system was new when we started. It's almost been over a decade, so maybe it's finally run its course. We won't be able to replace it until we can get a crew in here to work on it."

"Fine," Swann rubbed his bald head, "we are going to change course soon, so I would say the engine gets priority."

"I'll start on it," Reece stood up and handed his papers to Captain Swann.

Swann took the documents, and Reece left the room. Captain Swann looked out at the water. They had moved away from Zolis port and from Maine, all that could be seen was the calm ocean.

Navigation Room - 1:28 p.m.

The navigation room was dim, with the map the only light source. Terry, Mary, Crowe, and Koby stood around the map; the twins had changed into their regular outfits, while Crowe and Koby hadn't changed their clothes since last night. They all were looking at their new destination; Boston.

Terry straightened his vest, "why would they keep his body in Boston?"

"It's was the closest station when he was killed," Mary guessed.

"It happens to be near a port?" Koby's lab coat was pristinely clean and almost glowed.

"From what was seen," Crowe brushed her gray hair out of her face, "in the data. He was trying to get to the ocean. Most likely trying to get to one of the five ships."

"But no one said he contacted them?" Terry pointed out.

"We need to prepare for Boston," Crowe directed the conversation, "Ghost Shadow will be heading there. And we don't know what morgue in Boston he'll be in, so we'll have to find that out when we get there. But this time we won't have to break into an F.B.I. Station...just a police station. The police will have the information."

The mention of the hero made a chill go through the room.

"Terry," Crowe looked at the twins, "Mary, will you go tell the Captain. I believe he should be in his room."

"Sure," Terry said.

Terry and Mary walked out of the room.

Koby continued to look at the map, "you know, Hallowed might have been near Boston, waiting to pick Young up."

Crowe looked at Koby, "what makes you say that?"

"We haven't heard from them in months," Koby shrugged, "who knows what they've been doing?"

Main Deck – 1:43 p.m.

Terry and Mary walked along the deck. They decided to get some air before going to Captain Swann to report the data from the flash drive. The ocean shimmered with afternoon light, causing a glare upon its surface. Mary put a hand over her eyes to gaze out at the water. There was a creepy feeling, as she looked out across it, there wasn't any peace there for her.

Terry sighed dramatically, "do you think you'll be ready for Boston when the time comes?"

Mary looked at her brother, "I guess, what about you?"

Terry shook his head, "I don't want to do it, that's all I know right now... I don't want to do it!"

Confusion covered Mary's face, "why?"

"I'm tired of fighting," Terry clutched his hands into fists, "I don't even remember the reason for this fight. To me, there's no reason, other than fighting an apparition."

Mary stopped walking, while Terry continued down the ship. A distance grew between them.

Mary had once searched for the reason of the mission. And days like this one, she wished that she was still ignorant. She wished that some part of her was still unaware of what happened. Terry wasn't right. They weren't fighting an apparition, but a giant. They were just too close to see that.

Captain's Quarters — 2:04 p.m.

The room smelled as if it had recently been cleaned. Captain Swann sat in a chair at his table; his eyes scanned the documents. Chloe stood by the table, waiting for Swann's response.

"Pearson contacted you before they made it to the F.B.I. station and saw you?" Swann asked.

Chloe nodded, "he said he was coming with the hero and info."

Captain Swann sighed and read from the documents, "the resistance on land is dwindling. Many of the agents have been caught and put in jail. Replacement for agents has come to a standstill… How'd you know the watch was a data storage and have this information for us?"

"I gave it to him when we were dating, back in the Secret Service days" she explained.

A knock at the door ended the conversation.

Swann looked at the door, "come in."

Terry and Mary walked into the room, while Chloe exited.

"Hey Captain," Terry greeted.

"Terry," Swann smiled, "Mary, what's our destination?"

"Boston," Mary answered, "in Massachusetts."

"Good," Captain Swann rubbed his head, "we need to speak."

The twins shared a look.

"Is this about the peanut butter we took from Tegan?" Mary inquired.

Terry punched his sister in the arm.

"Ow," she complained.

Captain Swann eyed the two of them suspiciously, "we need to speak about what will happen in Boston. The two of you will have to see your father's body, to find the data."

"Oh," the twins said.

"No one else has the skills to find the data," Swann frowned, "I'm sorry we have to ask this of you."

"I don't get why this is a concern," Terry said, "we've accepted our father's death, and feel no need to dwell on it."

"Really?" Captain Swann paused and looked at both of them, "fine; you two can go. But make sure you return the peanut butter to Tegan."

The twins' expression changed to defeat, as they exited the room. Captain Swann felt like they hadn't been truthful, but they weren't ready to talk yet.

Mess Hall − 5:48 p.m.

Crowe sat down at one of the tables; she was the only one in the mess hall. Tegan walked in from the galley, or the kitchen as the twins called it. Tegan wore an apron over her clothes. She walked over to Crowe and sat down next to her crewmate.

"Do you remember when Young started this mission?" Tegan asked.

Crowe didn't look at Tegan, "yes, I was there with Captain Swann...I was there when it started. When everything went downhill."

Tegan nodded, "when he came to tell the staff, I was running the communications office. I didn't believe him at first, but then the news story hit, and there wasn't any denial after that."

Tegan fell silent.

"Are you worried about the twins?" Crowe gave her a sideways glance.

"Yes," Tegan sighed, "even if we get the data, will we be able to complete our duty?"

"Probably," Crowe shrugged, "it depends on what Young got before he died."

Tegan frowned, "and what about Terry and Mary?"

Crowe looked at the table, "there's a chance, if the data isn't useful, that they'll be consumed by their father's obsession or die. Their future isn't good... Even if the data is useful, we won't be able to use it right off. We'll probably have another ten years at sea."

Tegan frown deepened, "ironically they could use a hero."

The two woman sat in silence, wondering what would happen in Boston.

Chapter 7

Engine Room, May 28, 2106

- 8:55 a.m.

The engine room was in the stern of Lost Miracle.
It was a room full of pipes and grease. The tubes all
connected to the specialized engine. This engine used
very little gasoline and relied more on batteries. The air
was filled with a nasty smell from it all.

Reece walked around the room like he was on a
playground. He walked over to the main engine and
looked at the gears powering the ship. He was examining

the moving parts for any trouble. All the gears worked smoothly and moved mechanically. The only thing that was out of place was a high-pitched noise. Reece's ears could barely pick it up, but his eyes narrowed as his mind tried to figure it out.

The sound grew in volume, and his instinct made him back away. All at once the noise stopped. Replaced with an explosion of metal, grease, and steam. Reece slammed into a wall from the force of the blast.

All power in the ship went off, filling the rooms with darkness, as the ship came to a halt in the ocean.

"Crap," Reece muttered to himself.

He couldn't see anything in the dark room. He tried to stand, but a pain in his leg prevented him. Reece touched his leg and felt something sticking out with blood already bleeding out.

Doctor's Office – 9:36 a.m.

The doctor's office wasn't big and felt crowded when more than two people were in it. And even with Reece on the bed within the room, it still felt crowded. Koby stood by a cabinet against a wall, getting supplies for the wound in Reece's leg, Captain Swann stood in the corner, watching the doctor work on his crewmate.

The lights in the room were on from the generator. Reece's leg had been punctured by a piece of metal, luckily no bones or arteries had been hit. Koby had already removed the metal piece and stitched up the wound. He needed to give Reece a few shots of medicine before dressing it.

"So," Reece rested on his elbows, "how am I going to be? I still have the leg, so that's good."

Koby brought over his supplies and readied a needle, "you'll be fine. I'm putting antibiotics in you.

You'll need to keep off it for a week or two, maybe longer."

Captain Swann sighed, "that's good news...Reece, what about the engine?"

Reece leaned back on the bed, "the surge didn't damage the generator, but we're going to need spare parts from someone for the engine."

Swann narrowed his eyes, "I thought we got everything we needed at Zolis?"

"We did," Reece explained, "but an explosion like that causes damage that we weren't prepared for. We either need to go to shore or have one of the other ships help us."

Captain Swann nodded slowly, "very well, make a list and I'll arrange it."

Radio Room − 10:45 a.m.

The lights in the room were very dim, making it feel like desperate times. Even the radios were flickering from the surge that had happen. Crowe and Tegan both sat in the room with headsets over their ears.

"Please repeat Bala," Crowe said into a microphone, she pressed her headset into her ears.

Tegan twisted a dial, "okay, come in Gold Rose. We can hear you."

Both women listen to their lines as responses came in. The squeaks from the other side weren't recognizable expect in the headsets.

"Confirm Bala," Crowe switched stations, "Bala has no spare parts. And they won't be able to reach us, there on the west coast right now near Washington State."

Tegan turned her station off, "same for Gold Rose. No spare parts. Their ship has been tagged by the government too. So they've decided to go towards The Bahamas."

Crowe started searching for a new signal, "I'll try and make contact with Hallowed, they might have what we need."

Tegan snorted, "they never contact us, that ship has been missing for months, it's not worth trying anymore."

"Did you contact Blind Spirits?" Crowe continued her search on the radio.

"Yes," Tegan looked at her station, "they can't spare anything. Their ship has had problems. Their weapon system gave out last year, and they've been trying to fix it ever since. They're stuck within Hudson Bay in Canada."

Crowe shook her head, "I can't find Hallowed anywhere."

"Probably sank," Tegan suggested.

"You shouldn't joke," Crowe stood up, "I'll inform the Captain that the ships aren't coming to help."

Main Deck – 11:01 a.m.

The ship was still, even as small waves hit the sides, it seemed nothing could move the metal beast. The calm feeling was gone, and an eerie feeling covered the area. Crowe walked briskly across the deck, parallel to the railing. Swann was leaning on the railing looking up at the sky. There were several clouds, drifting by as if showing off that they could move.

"Captain!" Crowe called out.

Captain Swann glanced at her, "yes Crowe?"

"There's no help coming from the ships," she stood by him, she could feel the coldness coming from the water.

"So," Captain Swann turned his gaze back to the ocean, "we're going to shore?"

"Yes," Crowe nodded, "the nearest town is called Krafta, its barely in the state of New Hampshire. Who should go for supplies?"

Captain Swann pushed off the railing and stood up, "Chloe and you."

"Really?" Crowe looked skeptical.

Swann smiled, "yes, we need to get a list from Reece as soon as possible. Then you and Chloe can go to shore to retrieve the items...You haven't been to shore for six months; you need to take a break from the ocean."

"You haven't been to land for eight months," Crowe pointed out.

"Yeah," Swann said, "but I can handle the ocean, I served in the navy before I worked for Young, so I have an advantage."

Swann and Crowe started walking towards the tower.

Speedboat - 12:25 p.m.

The speedboat was on the starboard deck. Terry and Mary were filling the boat with supplies. Crowe and Chloe were leaving around midnight, so everything had to be ready that day. Mary was sorting items on the boat, while Terry viewed a checklist on the ship's deck. They had already loaded a couple of bags on.

"Do you think they will be able to get everything Reece needs?" Terry asked he glanced up at his sister.

Mary stretched her back, "most likely. Reece's writing isn't as bad as Koby's chicken scratch."

Terry laughed at his sister's joke. She jumped out of the boat and looked at the list Terry held. It wasn't a long list and was more of a checklist to make sure the boat was working and ready for the voyage.

"I believe we've finished checking," she stated.

"Yeah I agree," Terry looked at the vessel, "they won't be back until tomorrow morning, Krafta Coast is about three to four hours away from us. So it's going to be a long night."

"Do you think Reece will be able to fix the ship?" Mary asked.

"No," Terry yawned.

Mary gave her brother a disappointed look, "thanks for the confidence."

"Sorry," Terry shrugged, "but the damage is serious. We don't have any power right now, except the generator and it can't power the motors."

"But Reece has worked miracles before on the ship," Mary reminded him.

Terry yawned again.

Chapter 8

Krafta Coast, May 28, 2106

- 11:55 p.m.

Cold night air breathed across the ocean and land. The speedboat skimmed across the black surface of the water. Chloe steered the boat towards the dark coastline. She was making sure that they were near the port but not close enough to be seen. Crowe watched the coast as they neared it. Chloe slowed the boat and killed the engine as they came to the beach.

Crowe grabbed a backpack and jumped out of the boat to the sand. She started to pull the boat up onto the beach. Chloe picked her own bag up and joined Crowe. The two of them stabled the vessel so that it wouldn't float away.

"Where are we going first?" Chloe asked, they walked away from the boat and towards the town of Krafta.

"We are going to locate a tool shop, then go from there," Crowe explained, "I viewed the information stored about this town from a few years ago, they have several shops that we can scavenge from."

The duo crept through the night. Very few lights were on in the town, with just streetlights showing the way. It was hard to see any of the buildings, but they knew what direction they needed to go. Crowe had memorized all the data on Krafta, and Chloe was on alert.

Chloe wasn't nervous. She had training that prepared her for infiltration. Crowe didn't have the same training. Her skills had been about defending a person's interest, politically. She could navigate political waters better, than the ocean waves.

Krafta Town, May 29, 2106

- 12:36 a.m.

Krafta town wasn't big, but it still supported a strong community. They walked down a street, looking for a tool shop or mechanic's garage. The shops they passed were small. They usually were one-floor buildings with a simple set up; items in the front, employees in the back. It would have been nice to see the town in sunlight. The streetlights didn't give the beauty justice. It looked like a town from the 2030s.

"Do you think this town will have more than one tool shop?" Chloe asked.

"They should have more than one tool shop and mechanic's place," Crowe informed, "they have a college, that means they're a decent size, so."

"Good," Chloe muttered, she watched the area for any movement.

They continued down the street alone, as there wasn't anyone else out. Crowe directed them to a shop called William's Tool Box.

"This is our first stop," Crowe said.

Chloe walked to the side door of the building and started working on the lock. Crowe stayed on the street watching for trouble.

"I've got it," Chloe called over quietly, "do you think there's a security system?"

Crowe walked to her, "doubt it, there was hardly any crime here when we collected the data."

The two women walked into the dark shop.

Hammer Mechanics – 1:07 a.m.

Chloe picked the lock of the third store that night. The stores before had a couple of items that were needed, which were placed in Chloe's bag. This new shop, Hammer Mechanics, catered to cars and boats. Chloe unlocked the front door and opened it. The duo looked into the darkness of the building. They didn't see the flashing red light at the base of the door.

"We better go in," Crowe directed.

They turned their flashlights on as they entered. Crowe walked down a row full of cleaning supplies while Chloe had no luck in the next aisle. The items in the rows weren't useful. Crowe made her way out of the rows and briskly went to the main counter. She walked behind it and up to a door that said employees only. Opening the door, she saw several boxes.

"Chloe, storage is here!" Crowe called out.

Crowe pulled a box with the label boat towards her and opened it up. Inside was a big battery for a yacht. The battery was small for Lost Miracle, but Reece had said that he could make a smaller battery work. Chloe came over.

"I guess we could use that," Chloe commented.

Crowe packed it back up, and Chloe picked the box up.

"Reece should be able to modify it for the ship," Crowe suggested.

Chloe placed the box on the counter, "I'm going to take this back to the boat."

"Okay," Crowe nodded, "contact me when you're heading back."

Chloe left the shop with the box.

Streets of Krafta - 1:29 a.m.

Crowe sighed. She placed several mechanical parts into her backpack. The boxes in the storage room had been like buried treasure. Hammer Mechanics had a lot of pieces that were needed. Crowe felt she had gotten all the things on the list.

Headlights from a car beamed into the shop.

"Crap," Crowe grabbed her bag and covertly moved next to the front door.

The driver of the car turned the headlights off, got out of the vehicle, and walked up to the shop. A shadow of a big man entered the building cast by the streetlights. The shadow filled the shop with its presence. The door opened to the building, and the man walked in.

"Who's here?!" he yelled as the door slammed shut.

Crowe jumped the man. She put her arms around his neck. The man struggled against her, punching her in the face. But Crowe didn't let go and held fast. After several seconds the man went limp in her arms and collapsed onto her.

Crowe pushed the man off and stood up. She took keys out of his pocket and left the shop. She went to the car, opened the car door, sat down with her bag placed in the seat next to her, and started the vehicle. Backing the car up she turned it around and drove through the streets; taking out her phone, she dialed Chloe's number and waited for an answer.

Coastline – 1:41 a.m.

Crowe drove parallel to the ocean as she neared the spot of the speedboat. The car's headlights illuminated the dirt road she was taking. After knocking the shop owner out, she didn't want to be in Krafta anymore. Chloe hadn't picked up as Crowe tried calling her. The phone rang on speaker phone, as she waited for an answer.

The ringing stopped, "Crowe where are you?!"

Crowe drove the car onto the sand of the beach, "just coming up to the boat."

The headlights illuminated the area where the boat should have been. Nothing was there. The empty place was unexpected. Crowe stopped the car. She stared at the sand and dark water, waiting to see if it was an illusion.

"Where's the boat?!" Crowe didn't see any sign of the vessel.

"Don't know," Chloe answered.

"Why didn't you call!?" Crowe was staring at the empty beach in disbelief.

"I ran into a few problems," Chloe explained.

"Well, the owner of the shop came to the building, and I had to knock him out," Crowe glared, her anger was boiling, "we need to leave!"

"I'm at the port," Chloe explained, "I've gotten another boat ready."

"I'll be there in five," Crowe put the car in reverse.

She drove away from the beach and started going back to the city and port. Angry thoughts floated through her head. Crowe didn't understand why someone would take their boat, why someone would be out there in the first place, and why Chloe hadn't called.

Chapter 9

Krafta Port, May 29, 2106

- 1:58 a.m.

Crowe parked the car at Krafta Port. She grabbed her bag and stepped out of the vehicle. She gazed at the port, looking for Chloe. Several big sailboats were on the water among the wooden dock that extended out like a bar graph. Crowe walked down onto the dock. She held her phone in her hand waiting to see if it would vibrate. There was a docking house, but like most of the town, it didn't have a security system.

The water gently rocked the boats, causing them to look haunted in the darkness. Crowe's nerves were on high alert; but one boat caught her attention. It swayed more than the others. She walked to it quietly. If it wasn't Chloe, she didn't want to be seen.

The boat was bigger than the speedboat, but not by much. It looked as if it had a cabin with a sitting area. There were seats on deck for fishing, and written on the outside of the boat was the word Clinker.

"That's a terrible name," Crowe muttered.

Chloe, who had been in the cabin, walked out. Crowe jumped at suddenly seeing her crewmate appear.

Chloe looked at her, "how'd you know it was this one?"

Crowe shook her head, "you're rocking it."

Crowe tossed her bag up, and Chloe caught it, she untied the boat and climbed aboard. Making it rock more.

"Why this boat?" Crowe asked.

"The owner had just docked, and was walking away when I lifted his keys," Chloe took ahold of the steering wheel.

They drifted away from the wooden planks, towards the port's exit.

Lost Miracle, Radio Room

- 1:57 a.m.

In the darkness, the ship looked like a dark omen, waiting to take unexpecting boats to the bottom of the ocean. The inside of the ship wasn't as morbid. It was a trying time, but not a deadly one.

Tegan, Reece, and Koby sat in the radio room. Tegan worked at the radio listening to the law enforcement stations of Krafta. Koby wrote down the information Tegan received. Reece sat with his leg up, as

Koby was keeping an eye on him. The three of them had been there all night.

"Everything is still calm, nothing has happened in the small town," Tegan informed, she had one of her ears covered by the headset.

Koby made a notation, with Reece looking at his writing from across the table. He tried to read it upside down but was struggling.

"Your handwriting sucks," Reece observed.

Koby looked at him offended, "that's mean."

"Don't take it seriously," Tegan turned a dial, "he's full of drugs, remember?"

"Oh," Koby nodded, "right, you'll be able to read my handwriting when you're not medicated."

"I don't know about that," Reece muttered, "I'm pretty sure I couldn't read it before."

Tegan sat up straight as she relayed new information coming in, "local authorities have been alerted to a break-in and theft of a car. They are investigating the scene where a man was attacked and knocked unconscious. The authorities were alerted to it when he failed to check the alarm system."

Koby wrote down the information quickly, while Reece grabbed a phone on the table. He dialed Crowe's number and handed it to Koby. He took the phone from him and waited for the other line to pick up. It continued to ring.

Tegan tried to work the intercom system to contact the bridge and inform Swann, but failed to connect.

Clinker – 2:13 a.m.

The phone in Crowe's pocket vibrated. It tried to get Crowe's attention, for she hadn't heard it the first time because of the focus on trying to get out of Krafta Port.

The effort of trying to be quiet had made it hard to concentrate on anything else. But the vibration finally alerted her.

She answered it, "yeah?"

"The police are onto you," Koby said from the phone.

"Okay," Crowe said, "we lost the speedboat and are coming back in a different vessel. It's called the Clinker."

"We'll be ready for you," Koby hung up.

Crowe put her phone away. She stood on Clinker's deck, next to Chloe who steered the boat through the water. They had placed their items in the cabin of the vessel, so it was only them on the deck.

Chloe continued to guide the boat, "what's wrong?"

They drifted quietly among the other vessels tied to the dock. In the darkness the boats looked like wolves waiting to attack, making the Clinker feel like a scared sheep.

"The police have been alerted to our crimes in the town," Crowe informed.

Chloe sighed, "we'll be out to the ocean before they can track the car to the port, and find out that we stole a boat."

Crowe nodded. She looked at the parking lot, watching for any trouble. Her anger towards Chloe had quenched itself. She wanted to leave, and they were finally going.

Out at Sea - 2:21 a.m.

Chloe steered the Clinker out to sea. The dark water was a welcoming sight. Crowe watched the port shrink away. There hadn't been any alarms as they left.

The women stayed quiet, as they skimmed across the surface of the water. The spray from the ocean sprinkled in their faces. Getting them drenched a little as their speed caused waves to ripple out.

"Crowe!" Chloe called out.

"Yeah!" Crowe faced Chloe.

"I think I know what happened to the speedboat," Chloe commented.

They passed their speedboat in the water and saw a bunch of young adults on it. The young adults didn't notice the Clinker. They were too busy with their own thing. They wouldn't have even noticed Lost Miracle if it had gone by.

"What is the smell coming from them?" Chloe asked they continued through the water, they didn't stop.

"Well," Crowe shook her head, "there's a strong smell of alcohol. They must have spilled a whole barrel of something. Also maybe some weed."

Chloe snorted, "I'm glad we're leaving it."

Crowe smiled, "I wouldn't want to clean it after them."

They continued through the ocean towards Lost Miracle. The night air still had a cool breeze going across the surface of the black water and land. But the duo didn't notice the cold feeling. Their adrenaline made their blood warm.

Lost Miracle, Bridge - 2:38 a.m.

Koby ran into the bridge and tripped over his feet. He slammed to the floor and skidded across it. Captain Swann, who stood by the controls, watched his crewmate slide across the ground until he hit the other side of the room. The bridge's lights illuminated Koby's fall.

"You okay Doc?" Captain Swann asked.

"Yes," Koby pushed himself up to a seated position on the floor, "Crowe contacted us and informed us that they are coming back in a new vessel."

Swann helped Koby stand up.

"I came to tell you," Koby brushed himself off, "because we didn't want to use the intercom system."

"Okay," Swann looked at their controls, "the radar was picking up a vessel, but now I'm not worried about it. It seems to know right where we are, and no one else should know that."

"They weren't completely clean though," Koby continued to dust his lab coat off, "the police know they broke into a shop and stole a vehicle."

"So the police don't know its multiple shops?" Captain Swann summarized.

Koby nodded, "they aren't aware of everything."

"Get everyone to help with the boat when it comes in, then we will work in shifts to get the engine working again," Swann ordered, "we need to get this ship moving as fast as we can. We don't want the police from Krafta port to come looking for us, while we're a sitting duck."

Chapter 10

Lost Miracle, May 29, 2106

– 4:41 a.m.

Clinker slid smoothly next to the big black ship,

Lost Miracle. The crane on the deck moved until its

hooks dangled close enough for Crowe and Chloe to grab.

The two women both grabbed a hook. They clamped

them down on the stern and bow of the vessel, Clinker

became secure.

"Ready!" Chloe called out.

Crowe nodded and looked towards the railing of

Lost Miracle. Mary stood there watching. Crowe waved

at her, making Mary yell something towards the deck of the ship. The crane lifted the boat out of the water, and over the railing. Controls for the crane were meters away, with Terry at them. The controls reminded Crowe of an old arcade game with a claw and stuff animals.

The crane lowered the boat to the deck, with a little thud, as it was brought down. Chloe and Crowe instantly started collecting their things from the cabin of the boat. They handed their items to Mary, who stood there waiting for them. She received their box and bags.

"Did you get what was needed?" Mary asked.

Chloe and Crowe jumped down from the boat. They took their bags back and let Mary carry the box.

"For the most part," Chloe said.

"Where's the Captain?" Crowe inquired.

Mary pointed to the bridge. Crowe walked towards it, looking for Swann in the windows.

112

Radio Room - 7:54 a.m.

Tegan walked into the radio room and saw Crowe at one of the stations. She leaned back in her chair with a headset on listening. It was early in the morning with sunlight barely filtering into the room. Tegan walked over to her and placed a hand on her shoulder. Crowe looked up; she took the headset off.

"You should get some sleep," Tegan suggested.

Crowe nodded, "yeah, but I think I'll listen ten more minutes."

"Why ten?" Tegan sat down next to her.

"They found the car at the port," Crowe explained, "and they're finishing their investigation."

Tegan prepared the radio station in front of her. Turning dials, and flipping switches so power started going to it.

Crowe let out a sigh of relief, "they aren't suspicious enough to come out to open water. And still don't know about the boat missing. It will be awhile before they realize a boat was stolen. Probably won't be until the afternoon."

"Huh," Tegan placed a headset over her ears, "we're getting a message from Gold Rose."

Crowe watched Tegan listen to the report from the Gold Rose.

"Gold Rose confirmed Ghost Shadow's location," Tegan informed.

A sinking feeling filled Crowe at the mention of the hero's name.

"Thank you, Gold Rose," Tegan switched stations.

She looked at Crowe with distress written on her face.

"Don't tell me," Crowe sighed, "he's already in Boston. Waiting for us to be caught."

She nodded.

Bridge – 8:16 a.m.

Captain Swann looked out across the ocean through the windows. The windows were dirty, but they could still be seen through. Sunlight already danced across the water's surface. The view from the bridge was back to being beautiful and peaceful at the moment. It almost felt like the waves of the sea were cheering them on. But the clouds still gave off a bragging manner way up in the sky, away from gravity. Tegan walked up to the bridge and entered.

"Captain, we have news," Tegan stated, "they've come from the town of Krafta and Gold Rose ship."

Captain Swann faced his crewmate, "what's your report?"

"Krafta won't be coming out to open ocean, their investigation won't lead to us it looks like," Tegan informed, "but a new problem has risen. The hero, Ghost Shadow, is in Boston already waiting for us."

Swann nodded slowly, "so he'll be near the body."

Tegan observed Swann, "what are your orders?"

"They haven't changed," Captain Swann said, "we will continue as planned. But we will need to tell the crew about Ghost Shadow in Boston."

"Yes Captain, I will go inform everyone," Tegan left the room, she went down the ladder she had just come up.

Swann shook his head and sat down in the chair in front of the controls, the beauty around him had suddenly lost its glory.

Doctor's Office – 8:33 a.m.

Koby, Terry, Mary, and Reece were in the
doctor's office. Reece rested on the bed, while the twins
sat in chairs. Koby leaned against the wall watching.
Mary and Terry were listening to Reece as he explained
what needed to happen in the engine room.

"Make sure all the debris is cleaned away," Reece
explained, "you're also going to make sure the main
engine isn't leaking gas or liquids. If it is you'll need to
have Captain Swann or Koby help you stop the leaks."

"So we're just the cleanup crew?" Terry asked.

"Yes," Reece answered, "Captain Swann and
Koby will be down there with you fixing the engine. This
will be a complicated thing, so don't touch anything
unless you have too."

Mary and Terry both sighed at being given
cleanup duty.

Tegan opened the door; everyone turned their attention to her.

"I've come to inform the crew that Ghost Shadow is in Boston," Tegan announced.

The news stunned everyone, and they felt sick as the realization of the problem hit.

"Really?" Reece shook his head in frustration, "I figure he would get there sooner or later, now he's just going to camp on top of the morgue."

"Camp?" Mary asked.

"It's a gaming term," Koby explained.

"They camp in games?" Terry gave them a confused look.

"I have to go tell Chloe," Tegan left the room.

Navigation Room – 10:48 a.m.

Chloe stood in the navigation room. Tegan had informed her of the hero's location, and after that, she went to this room to look at the map. She held several papers that dictated the layout of Boston and the morgues there. The map was zoomed in on the Boston area. Knowing Ghost Shadow was there made sleep impossible.

There was no way of avoiding it. The hero was going to get another chance at the twins. Ghost Shadow knew there was a reason Ian Young's body was significant but probably didn't have the skills to figure out why. She wondered if someone else might have realized that they needed to look for something on the body, or if they were remaining quiet about what they knew?

Chloe shook her head. She continued to look at the layout of Boston. Looking for ways to get away if they had to use an escape route; there was a higher chance one would be needed. There was almost a guarantee that the hero would see them. But Chloe wasn't sure she would get the opportunity to surprise him again, the crew wasn't that lucky.

Captain Swann knew her concerns, but he didn't have a solution. Chloe shifted her gaze from the map, back to the documents she had collected. They listed all the buildings and streets in Boston. She focused on the part of the list that held three different morgues on it. One of them held Ian Young's body; they just didn't know which one.

Chapter 11

Engine Room, June 3, 2106

- 4:23 p.m.

Several days had gone by with engine room out of commission, but the smell of years out on the ocean didn't go away that easily. The smell of the room hadn't grown weaker; it had grown stronger.

Reece limped around the pipes and grease on the floor. Mary stood next to him shining a flashlight on the ground, so he could see where he was going. Terry stood on the other side of the engine, holding a different flashlight directed towards the engine. The twins had been helping him work like this for a couple of hours. They had to turn off all the power in the ship, just in case an overload happened to the circuit.

"We're almost done," Reece informed the twins.

Terry sighed, "it's only taken five days."

"Four," Mary corrected, "and Reece hasn't been able to be here the whole time."

"Terry, move your light to the left," Reece directed.

Terry shifted his beam, and Reece knelt down. He held a wrench and started working. After several minutes, he stood back up on his good leg.

"Mary will you go to the breaker box," Reece pointed to it on the wall, "and flip the main switch."

Mary walked over and opened the breaker box. She flipped the main switch at the top. The sound of buzzing filled the air, and a couple of sparks jumped off of the engine's new battery. Power slowly returned to the engine. The motors underneath started to hum. The movement could be felt as the metal beast moved once again through the water of the vast ocean.

Bridge – 4:38 p.m.

The lights were at full power. Captain Swann watched the ship come back to life and move through the ocean from the bridge. The sudden movement from being so still gave the ship a greater presence in the water. It felt like a titan had awakened, coming to rule the world.

As they moved through the water, Swann adjusted their course. Twisting dials on the control panel and moving the helm. It clicked into place, and Captain Swann was able to let go. The automatic part of the ship hadn't been affected by the explosion. They were on their way to Boston Port. Swann sighed to himself as he directed his crew closer to the dangerous enemy. Going towards trouble was never a smart thing to do, but it wasn't a choice anymore.

His nerves were uneasy, sweat formed on his head and the back of his neck. Swann sat down and watched the ocean go by, trying to keep himself calm. His mind wouldn't let him rest; it reminded him of the threat coming.

Captain Swann placed his head in his hands; focusing on controlling his breathing. Going back ten years, he would have never thought this was where he would be. To him, it hadn't even been a possibility. But when something terrible happens, something becomes terribly changed.

Mess Hall – 4:54 p.m.

Crowe walked into the mess hall. Tegan and Koby sat at one of the tables having a snack of popcorn. Crowe walked over to them and sat down.

"I need a favor," Crowe said.

Koby and Tegan looked at her; they continued to eat their popcorn. They waited for Crowe to tell them the favor.

"Do you think you could come up with a medical reason for the twins not to go to Boston?" Crowe asked Koby.

"Yes," Koby snorted, "but it's based on what could happen to them, not on anything current, so really I couldn't."

Crowe sighed and placed her head on the table, "they shouldn't have to deal with Ghost Shadow again…Can't you make something up?"

Koby didn't answer Crowe as he stood up, "I have to check on Reece."

Koby left the room. Tegan started packing their food away.

"I understand," Tegan started, "you considered the twins your kids, but you need to let them do this. We have no other choice, and it's not just their future on the line."

Crowe lifted her head from the table, "I know. I just can't believe we've come down to this…We were supposed to work for eight years together, then move on. But it's been over ten."

Tegan considered Crowe, "you can quit anytime, but we both know that ten years ago, you became the most dedicated person for this cause."

Tegan left the room. Crowe shook her head, before laying it back on the table, her gray locks spilling around her.

Navigation Room – 5:16 p.m.

Terry and Mary were the only ones in the navigation room. They examined the map; looking at the path they were taking to Boston across the ocean. Mary stood back, while Terry leaned over the map.

"Mary," Terry whispered, "are we going to end up like Father and Mother?"

Mary considered, "no."

"Your reason?" Terry inquired, he looked at his sister.

"We have Lost Miracle," she answered simply, "Father didn't have anyone there to help out, and well,

Mother…it was completely out of the blue. No one knew it was coming."

Terry looked back at the map. Mary stepped up and stood next to her brother. The two of them focused on Boston.

Terry nodded slowly, "do you think anyone cried when he died? I know it's been years since he was President of the nation, but do you think they remembered him?"

Mary frowned, "I bet the nation wept because of his death; they would never forget him…they knew he would have never betrayed them…They knew he was always fighting for them. I think the only person who doesn't know that is Ghost Shadow…I wonder if he's even American. It would make sense if he weren't, then he wouldn't have known really who Father was. And would have had no problem doing his mission."

"I bet that's true," Terry agreed, "that might be why he didn't think about Chloe back at Zolis, or the fact that he didn't realize who we were at first."

Crew Quarters – 6:39 p.m.

Koby examined Reece's leg as he laid on the bottom bunk. The crew quarters were two rooms each had two sets of bunk beds in each room, one on each side, with a drawer for every individual against a wall. Koby sat on a stool while he worked. Chloe laid on the top bunk. The men didn't know if Chloe was awake or asleep.

"I'm not in any bad pain," Reece informed Koby, he watched the doctor examine him.

Koby unwrapped his leg and cleaned the wound, "that's good, and you're taking care of it, right?"

"Yes, Doc," Reece answered promptly.

Koby focused on the wound. It had healed in the last few days and looked healthy.

"Good," Koby bandaged the leg again, "I know it's early, but you should get some rest."

"Okay, will you turn the lights off?" Reece shifted in his bed.

"Yeah, goodnight," Koby turned the lights off and left.

The room was dark with a small light shining on the floor so people could see in the dark. The creaking of the ship lulled Reece to sleep. Chloe, though, didn't sleep as her thoughts of Boston kept her up. She went over the movements of the hero and handler in her mind from the attack in Zolis. It was all she had to work with to prepare herself for the coming mission and duty. She had known Pearson, but that was over a decade ago. And she wasn't sure what he could do for them. He had to keep up appearances so his cover wouldn't be questioned.

The moving of the ship swayed; the room felt like a carriage, rocking back and forth.

Chapter 12

Outside of Boston, June 8, 2106 − 8:38 a.m.

The engine of Lost Miracle turned off; the ship slowly stopped moving through the water. The port of Boston could be seen on the horizon. In the morning light, the city looked hopeful to some people. Captain Swann stood in the bridge looking at the city; he wasn't happy.

He watched with his arms folded against his uniform that was fresh and pressed. He looked like a real captain. He wasn't happy to see the city but was glad they had made it. The weather hadn't been giving them any trouble, and appeared to be where all their luck was going. Koby walked into the bridge and up to Swann.

"Should we prepare a departure for Boston?" Koby inquired.

Swann nodded, "the time has ticked down. We need to get ready within a half-hour."

Koby turned to leave, but Swann stopped him.

"Make sure Chloe, the twins, and Crowe are the ones on the boat," Captain Swann added, "I want all four of them."

Koby nodded before leaving to find his crewmates. He walked down the ladder from the bridge. He reentered the ship from a door at the base of the tower.

Swann focused back on Boston. The port was almost like a jewel on the horizon, with its place right in the center.

Clinker - 9:03 a.m.

Terry and Mary climbed onto the Clinker's deck. They both had plain t-shirts with jeans and a baseball cap covering their heads. Chloe wore an outfit like the twins with a jacket, as she stood on Lost Miracle's deck next to the boat. Crowe stood next to her in a similar outfit too.

"So you expect people to think we're a family?" Chloe handed a backpack to Terry on the boat.

"Something like that," Crowe climbed aboard the Clinker.

Chloe shook her head at Crowe's reasoning. They looked like tourists that would stand out anywhere they went. But Crowe was in-charge of the mission, so Chloe and the twins had to listen.

"Ready!" Mary called out; she finished going over the boat.

Chloe nodded, she looked at the controls for the crane. Tegan stood behind the controls. She waited to get the all clear.

Chloe climbed aboard the Clinker and gave Tegan the signal. She controlled the crane making it move the boat into the air, over the railing of Lost Miracle and into the water lightly. Clinker was released, and allowed to drift in the water.

Chloe started up the engine and took control of the steering. Clinker sprang to life and shot out across the water. Going straight to Boston. They weren't going at an angle or trying not to be seen. Their destination was the port.

Boston Port – 10:24 a.m.

Chloe slowed the boat as it entered the port. The dock was a lively place. People worked on their boats and walked along the wooden planks. The sunlight was strong and danced in between the vessels with the water.

Terry and Mary looked at the names of the boats as they

passed by. Several boats were advance, with very little of

the vessel in the water. But there were still some like

Clinker that floating around.

"Is that one called Sundew?" Terry pointed at an

old sailboat.

Mary looked at the boat, "what's a sundew? A

fruit or a flower?"

"I bet a hippy owns that boat," Terry guessed, "or

a biologist. I could see a biologist naming their boat

Sundew."

"Really," Mary's face was covered with confusion.

Crowe and Chloe focused on finding a place to

dock the boat. They neared a space, as Chloe turned the

engine off. Clinker gradually drifted next to the dock. A

silent sensor went off, signaling to the docking house that

the slot was filled. Crowe jumped onto the wooden planks and tied their boat. Their vessel looked normal among the other boats at the port. There wasn't anything usual about their boat, and Crowe was relieved.

"Remember we need to blend in," Chloe reminded the twins.

The twins gave her confused looks.

"Yeah wearing the same outfit will help that," Terry said sarcastically.

Mary sighed at her brother's remark.

Chloe took the key out of the ignition. Mary grabbed her bag and stepped onto the wooden planks. Terry followed after with Chloe behind him. The four of them walked down the planks, towards the city.

Docking House – 10:37 a.m.

The smell of fish guts covered the entire area in a thick aroma. It was powerful when passing the fishing boats along the dock. Chloe led the group up the planks towards the docking house. The house looked like a shack, but it still had a friendly exterior with flowers in the window seal and very clean outside with solar panels lining the roof.

"Terry, will you come in with me?" Chloe asked.

"Why?" Terry smirked.

"You're a charmer," Chloe dragged Terry into the shack.

Crowe and Mary watched them go into the small building. They went up to the counter and started talking to a man behind it.

"So are you my mother or aunt? Or even my weird neighbor from across the street?" Mary asked, "since we're trying to be a family."

"Do you think Chloe could be your mother?" Crowe watched Chloe talking to the man as she paid him for their spot.

Mary considered, "no, I guess you're my mother, and she's the crazy aunt."

Crowe smiled, "don't tell her that. She doesn't like to be called crazy."

Chloe and Terry walked out of the shack.

"We're set," Chloe announced, "there shouldn't be any trouble with our boat."

"Did they recognize you?" Crowe asked.

"No," Chloe shook her head, "I don't think they did or they didn't care."

The small group walked away from the docking house and towards the city.

Streets of Boston – 11:21 a.m.

The streets of Boston were alive and full of activity. People rushed down the sidewalks as they started early on their lunch breaks. The Lost Miracle group merged with the crowd.

Crowe led them along the sidewalk, as she went over the map mentally in her head. She knew right where they were and which way they needed to go. There was precision in the way they moved through the city. Crowe stopped them in front of a café with an outside seating arrangement.

"We'll rest here and wait for the noon hour," Crowe sat down at one of the tables in the café, "then go to the police station."

They all sat around the table. It was tiny, but the four of them still manage to fit. Salt and pepper with napkins in-between greeted them, with a call button for the waiter. A digital menu popped up within the table, allowing customers to select what they wanted.

"How much farther?" Chloe asked.

"A block," Crowe answered, "it isn't that far."

The café was almost full, but they blended in.

"Do you think the hero will be there?" Mary whispered.

"Don't know," Chloe answered truthfully.

Terry patted Mary's shoulder, "probably not. Don't worry we have our crazy aunt to look after us."

Terry smiled at Chloe. She glared back at him but didn't say a word. Crowe finally smiled at one of Terry's jokes.

Chapter 13

City of Boston, June 8, 2106

- 12:04 p.m.

Skyscrapers filled Boston, it was all business in

this area. The buildings shimmered and stood against the

sunlight. These high-tech buildings made the world

around feel out of place; like they were the gods

watching.

The lunch hour had begun, a race to get food

started. Everyone filed out of buildings and filled the

sidewalks, all heading towards desirable places. The Lost

Miracle group used the crowd as cover to get closer to the police station.

The small group was unaware of the danger coming as they continued down the sidewalk. The two men from Zolis port, hero and handler, stepped onto the sidewalk. The men went with the flow of the people, towards the small group. They were unaware of their prey coming up to them, and both groups were overwhelmed by the number of people.

Ghost Shadow still wore the black coat that was too big for him. It was shocking the small group didn't notice him as they passed in the crowd. He didn't blend in with his surroundings and the unnatural feeling continued to follow him.

The handler, Pearson, walked behind the hero and his eyes caught the movement of the crew. He tried to catch sight of them again, but they disappeared before he could see them. The crowd continued to push him forward.

He didn't stop walking with Ghost Shadow, but he continued to look back as they made their way down the street. His instinct didn't let him forget the sight of his prey.

Police Station - 12:11 p.m.

The four of them walked around the front of the police building and to the side alley. Chloe took out her skeleton key card from a pocket for the alley door to the police station. Terry sent a virus at the single camera in the alley, interrupting the feed for twenty minutes. The group didn't have to worry about being noticed. She opened the door, and her fellow crewmates walked into the building. Terry and Mary walked behind Crowe as she led them to the main room of the station. Computers and desks filled the area. There wasn't any crisis going on, as officers walked casually around. Thankfully it was a slow today.

Terry and Mary walked up to one of the desks and started working on the computer. With Terry typing and Mary plugging in her laptop to add support. There weren't very many people in the station at the moment, but Chloe and Crowe kept watch as people walked around. They did get strange looks, but everyone was too self-absorbed to think twice about the four of them. It was risky going to the police station during the day, but it was completely unexpected to find the Lost Miracle crew there.

"We have confirmed that they stored his body at the Goodrest morgue," Mary informed, "that's where the police keep all their bodies."

"Getting directions now," Terry added.

Crowe nodded. Mary unplugged her laptop and put it away. Terry finished and turned the computer off.

"Let's go," Chloe led them back the way they had come.

They went back down the hall and towards the alley door. No one noticed the four fugitives.

Parking Lot - 12:36 p.m.

The four of them walked out of the police station from the same alley door. They walked to the street and went two blocks away before stopping to gather themselves. They didn't run, but their hearts pounded. Their bodies felt like they had been fleeing from a monster.

"We need to go east," Terry informed, "the morgue is just a couple of blocks away, maybe a mile at most."

"Okay," Crowe continued to look for anyone following them.

Chloe's eyes turned to a grocery store's parking lot. The lot was full of cars shining in the sunlight.

"Let's get a ride," Chloe walked over to the parking lot.

"Do we have to steal now?" Mary followed with the others, "we don't want attention. And it's really rude to take someone's car at a grocery store."

Chloe put a small device on the door handle of a car, after several seconds it opened the door disarming the alarm. She opened the door quickly, and hot-wired the vehicle, starting the engine. The car was ready for use. She sat in the driver's seat.

"Mary, our outfits catch people's attention," Terry mumbled, "we don't need alarms to point us out. We do that ourselves."

Crowe, Mary, and Terry got into the car. Chloe drove them out of the parking lot before the driver of the vehicle could come to see it driving away.

Streets of Boston – 12:55 p.m.

Chloe drove respectfully down the street, which was unusual for her driving. Terry and Mary looked out the windows watching the city go by. Crowe watched them through the side mirrors. The four of them almost looked like a family going to the beach or a museum.

"It's weird going the speed limit," Mary mumbled to herself.

"It's weird not being chased," Terry pointed out.

The twins smirked at each other for their witty comments.

Crowe sighed and turned in her seat to face them, "we need to talk about the morgue."

The twins looked at her funny. Crowe gave them a concerned look back, with Chloe looking at them through the rearview mirror. They looked like they were having a staring contest.

"You're about to see your father's dead body," Crowe gave them a comforting smile, "it's going to be hard. Seeing a loved one's body in normal circumstances is hard, but going to a morgue because they've been murdered is another level of difficulty."

"Crowe," Terry sighed, "it's just going to be another dead body to us. We weren't close to our father."

Mary nodded, "we haven't seen him for two years. The crew is more family to us than he was. I mean if I saw your dead body, I would freak out...But our father didn't feel like family."

Silence followed their words. Crowe turned back in her seat to face the front. Her concern deepened.

Goodrest Morgue - 1:17 p.m.

The small group, dressed in their matching outfits, stood outside the morgue looking at the building. The building was square like all the others in the area and didn't stand out. The four of them were almost expecting it to be a fort and were a little disappointed at its lack of uniqueness. They walked to the side of the building and to a side door; it could be seen from the street, but there weren't any cameras for the building. Chloe went up to the door and started working on the lock. But she found it difficult. Chloe could barely move the pins inside; the bolt had rusted.

"Chloe, we can't keep standing here," Terry urged, he looked at the street nervously

"I'm trying," Chloe said through gritted teeth.

Crowe looked down the alley and walked to the back of the building. She disappeared from view. The others didn't notice her departure. Everyone grew in concern as the seconds continued to go by. Chloe worked frantically to move the pins in the lock. She slammed her hand on the door in anger, causing her lock pick tools to scatter to the ground.

"Crap," she hurriedly picked them up.

The side door swung open, surprising everyone. Crowe stood on the other side. Holding the door open, waiting for them to enter.

"How the heck?" Terry couldn't believe her.

"Saw someone going out of the building," Crowe ushered them in, "so I snuck in, just before the door closed."

The twins and Chloe entered the morgue.

Chapter 14

Autopsy Room, June 8, 2106

- 1:29 p.m.

A fire alarm rang throughout the morgue, causing everyone to exit the building, but the Lost Miracle crew didn't take heed of it for they had pulled the alarm. The four of them entered the autopsy room. The room had a chill and a robust sterile smell. One operation table was in the middle of the room, with a low hanging light. Several medical machines filled the area, with places for more tables to rise from the floor. Metal containers lined the back wall, steel boxes embedded within.

Chloe walked over; she started opening the boxes. Crowe assisted by working on the other side. The twins watched as they made their way through the dead bodies of random people. They found Ian Young's body at the center of the wall. Crowe opened a container. The body had a sheet over it, and Crowe revealed his face.

"I found him," Crowe announced.

The fire alarm rang in everyone's ears, but her announcement made them stand still. Ian Young's body had become a reality. Crowe took a step back, Chloe closed her container, and the twins walked slowly up to the body.

Ian Young's skin was pale, and his short black hair was messy. His face looked peaceful with his eyes closed. Terry and Mary peered at their father. They had become solemn. It may have been years since they had seen him alive, but nothing could counter seeing him dead for the first time.

"You two okay?" Crowe asked.

"Yeah," Terry mumbled.

Chloe pulled out pliers from Mary's bag, "let's find the data."

Crowe opened Ian Young's mouth.

Goodrest Morgue – 1:46 p.m.

"I think I've found it!" Terry held up a tooth; he yelled even though the fire alarm had finally been turned off.

Chloe stopped pulling teeth out, as everyone looked at the tooth Terry held. The tooth was different from the pile of teeth on Young's chest. It was fake with a screw poking out of the bottom.

"How'd you miss that Chloe?" Crowe inquired.

"I went into a zone," Chloe answered.

Crowe and Chloe looked at the pile of teeth on the dead body. There wasn't very much blood, but the collection was unnerving.

Mary took out a device to hunt for data, "it's searching."

The device locked onto the data found within the tooth. It showed several data clumps within.

"We've got it!" Mary announced.

"Finally," Chloe wiped the pliers off and put them away.

Terry put the tooth in a plastic baggy before putting it in Mary's bag.

"Let's get going; we don't want to stay here!" Crowe rushed to the door with the others behind her.

They entered the hallway but stopped at the doorway.

"I need to check," a man's voice echoed.

"And the hero?" another voice asked.

"Coming," the first man answered.

The Lost Miracle crew watched Pearson, and a doctor turned the corner. Pearson locked eyes with the crew, as both realized the situation they were in.

"Pearson," Chloe mumbled.

"Run," Crowe ordered

The crew ran, with Pearson giving chase, leaving the doctor behind.

Morgue Parking Lot - 1:55 p.m.

Crowe rushed into the parking lot underneath the morgue. Terry and Mary followed. The three of them started a chain reaction. Crowe tripped over her feet, crashing to the ground. Terry and Mary didn't stop, piling on top of Crowe. The three of them became a human knot.

"Ow," Crowe yelped.

"Sorry," Terry called out.

"Crowe, you're pulling my hair," Mary complained.

The three of them struggled against each other on the asphalt.

Chloe appeared in the doorway, as Pearson tackled her into the parking lot, barely missing the others. Crowe and the twins watched them roll away.

"We need to help," Crowe tried to untangle herself.

Chloe and Pearson scraped against the asphalt, giving each other road rashes. Crowe kicked the twins off, and rushed to Chloe joining the wrestling.

"Ow," Terry cried.

Chloe and Crowe pinned him to the ground. Chloe placed her foot in the middle of his back. Crowe held onto his legs.

"Okay," Chloe breathed heavily.

The adults looked dirty and messy. Their hair frizzy, and their clothes filthy. Terry and Mary untangled themselves and stood up.

"You two are awesome," Terry commented.

"Not bad for your crazy aunt," Chloe smirked.

"Mary, check his pockets," Crowe breathed heavily too, "we need his keys."

Mary looked in his pocket and got the keys out.

"Find his car," Crowe directed.

The twins started searching the parking lot.

Rental Car – 2:11 p.m.

Terry drove Pearson's rental car. Mary sat in the front seat; she watched the backseat where the adults sat. Pearson sat in the middle with his hands tied in front. Crowe sat on his right and Chloe on his left. The three of them still had dirt on their faces and clothes.

"What's with you people?" Pearson asked he was bleeding from a cut on his right shoulder that bled through his shirt.

"The sidekick speaks," Mary mumbled.

"I'm not a sidekick," he mumbled back.

"What are you?" Crowe asked she pushed a lock of gray hair behind one of her ears.

"A babysitter," he answered honestly.

"That sucks," Chloe commented, "having an assignment like that is a draining one with little reward. But you already knew that."

"Where are you taking me?" he asked, directing the conversation.

"Port," Crowe answered.

"You shouldn't tell him," Terry protested, he glanced at them from his shoulder.

"He's not blindfolded," Mary pointed out to her brother.

The twins gave each other strange looks as they realized he was aware of their surroundings.

"Shouldn't he be blindfolded?" Terry asked.

"No," Chloe sighed, "the port is too unique. Also, we might be pushing him into the water, so he'll need his eyes for that."

"Really?" Pearson asked.

Chloe nodded.

"What's your name?" Crowe asked, "I don't remember."

"Stanley Pearson," he answered.

"No hero name," Terry joked.

No one laughed.

Morgue - 2:15 p.m.

Ghost Shadow, in his black coat, stared at Ian Young's body. The teeth sat on his chest in a pile. He wasn't unnerved by the mutilation done, he had grown used to that in prison. The head doctor watched the hero from the doorway; he didn't want to be closer to him. The rumors of Ghost Shadow coming from human experimentation scared him.

"Pearson ran after the people?" Ghost Shadow glanced at the doctor.

"Yes," he said nervously.

Ghost Shadow rubbed his shaven head. He sighed and turned away from the dead body. He walked out of the room with the doctor by his side going down the hallway.

"To the parking lot?" Ghost Shadow inquired.

"Yes," the doctor answered promptly.

The two of them exited the morgue and entered the parking lot underneath the building. There were scuffs on the asphalt from the fight, but not much else. It was quiet, with the cars of the employees lined up waiting to be chosen by their owners.

"After you called the police," Ghost Shadow knelt down, "you didn't see Pearson again?"

"Correct," the doctor nodded.

"Thank you, doctor," Ghost Shadow stood up.

"What about the teeth?" the doctor inquired.

"Don't know," Ghost Shadow faced the parking lot's exit.

Five thick black coils emerged from his coat pockets. The doctor recoiled in fear. The five coils moved in a fluid motion. They lifted him off the ground, like spider legs. He went out of the parking lot in a graceful motion. The doctor fainted from shock.

Chapter 15

Lost Miracle, Bridge Deck, June 8, 2106 – 2:36 p.m.

Swann looked at Boston on the horizon. He hadn't moved from the bridge since the group left. He waited for any signs of a struggle to show up. The port of Boston was targeted on Lost Miracle's defense system. A computer screen on a control panel had the seaport magnified; the screen showed what boats were going in and out. He would watch the screen as he rotated his gaze from the horizon.

"Captain," the intercom system squealed painfully.

Captain Swann walked over to the speaker and flipped a switch, "Doctor?"

"Got a message from Chloe, Tegan is bringing it to you, she'll be there soon," Koby informed.

"Thank you," Swann turned the intercom off.

After a few minutes, Tegan walked to the bridge and entered the room.

"Captain," she greeted.

"The message?" Swann inquired.

"They kidnapped the handler for protection against Ghost Shadow," she relayed, "and they're taking him to the port. They aren't sure if he'll be on the boat with them. They haven't seen Ghost Shadow yet, so it's unclear."

Captain Swann nodded, "prepare the defense system. We might have to defend them."

"Yes sir, I'll help Reece," Tegan paused, "when do you think you'll fire?"

Swann gestured to the image of the port on the screen, "when I see the boat coming through the water."

Tegan nodded, "yes sir."

"Make sure he gets both systems working," Captain Swann reminded her.

She acknowledged his reminder, and left Swann alone, as she exited the bridge.

"So they have Pearson," Swann mumbled to himself.

City of Boston - 2:39 p.m.

The city of Boston sparkled beautifully in the sunlight. Skyscrapers shimmered, bouncing light around, with streets full of cars driving along with sidewalks full of people gave the city a lively feeling. Several small apartment buildings were scattered throughout the city with business buildings mixed in. There was also a fresh breeze twisting through. It felt like a well-rounded area.

Ghost Shadow stood on top of a tall apartment building. In his black coat, he looked like a vulture waiting for his prey. He searched the streets with his eyes. It was highly unlikely he would see Pearson's car, but he had a hunch that they were going towards the ocean. With Lost Miracle out there, he knew the sea was where they wanted to be.

Tracking them wasn't his strength, that was why he had Pearson around. But with him being kidnapped. He had to assume they were going to the port and not another place.

He let a sigh escape. The black tentacles uncoiled from his coat pockets once again. The tentacles gripped the side of the building with finger-like dexterity, and Ghost Shadow swung off. The black coils maneuvered him to the next building.

A beeping sound caught his attention from within his pants' pocket. He took out the phone making the noise, while still moving between buildings. The name Bergen was on the screen.

He ignored the call.

Port of Boston - 2:47 p.m.

Chloe and Crowe held Pearson, while the five of them walked down the dock. Pearson didn't cause any trouble, as Chloe held her gun to his back. He didn't realize it was the stun gun.

"Terry," Chloe ordered, "Mary, look for the boat."

The traffic had increased in the port, with several bigger vessels being on the water making it hard to spot a smaller boat.

"It's here somewhere," Terry looked frantically around.

Mary glanced behind, stumbling on the planks and falling.

"You okay?" Crowe asked.

Terry helped her stand, as Mary pointed behind them towards the parking lot.

"Problem," Mary stated.

Everyone turned around. Ghost Shadow had placed himself on the docks, with his coils disappearing into his pockets.

"I want my sidekick!" he ordered.

Terry and Mary hid behind the adults, still looking for the boat.

"Don't get closer," Crowe warned.

"He doesn't like being called a sidekick," Chloe pointed out.

Crowe and Pearson gave Chloe a weird look.

"If you hurt him, I will come at you like a raging bull," Ghost Shadow stated.

"Bull?" Chloe smirked, "are we in Madrid?"

"He's never been to Europe," Pearson mumbled, "he won't get the joke."

Terry's eyes locked onto the Clinker, "found it."

The twins ran to the boat. Mary untied the boat. The twins both got on, as Terry started it up. They moved it closer to Crowe and Chloe.

Ghost Shadow took out three black tentacles, they arched over his head and formed into sharp points. Chloe took her gun out from Pearson's back and fired at the hero. An electrical current zapped through the air, hitting the hero in the shoulder, causing a tentacle to liquefy and splash onto the dock.

He struck out with the other two. One lodged into the wooden planks of the dock, and the other hit Chloe's arm. She dropped her gun at the sudden pain.

Crowe pushed Pearson onto Clinker's deck and ran to Chloe's aid. The black tentacle held fast, as its point embedded into Chloe's arm.

Ghost Shadow pulled his other tentacle out of the dock, getting it ready to strike.

Crowe came up and kicked the tentacle connecting Chloe to the hero. It shattered releasing

Chloe. The two women ran down the dock and onto

Clinker.

"Drive," Crowe ordered.

Terry took the steering wheel and accelerated.

Ghost Shadow reacted quickly, he struck the boat with a

tentacle, but the boat pulled away, breaking the

connection. The coil shattered, turning to a black liquid

that sprayed everywhere. The Clinker zoomed away from

the dock and hero. Ghost Shadow continued to shoot

black shards at them from the wooden planks, splattering

the boat with more black liquid.

Clinker – 3:02 p.m.

Terry steered the boat away from the dock. The

tentacle's liquid became slimy. It covered everything.

Mary held onto her brother as they left Ghost Shadow

behind. The water between them was a lifesaver.

"What are those black tentacles?" Crowe asked, she reached into Mary's bag and got the first aid kit out.

Terry moved the boat out of the port and into deeper water, putting even more distance from the hero.

"Ink," Pearson explained, he sat calmly as Crowe bandaged Chloe's arm.

Chloe grimaced through the pain. Crowe finished bandaging and took over driving, changing the angle, so they were going towards Lost Miracle.

"Ink, his name is Ghost Shadow," Mary looked confused, she still held onto her brother for comfort.

"I know it doesn't make sense," Pearson mumbled, "they were trying to make him seem more threatening with that name."

"You're not happy," Chloe observed, she held her arm gingerly.

"I've been kidnapped," Pearson gave Chloe a weird look again, "you think I should be cheering for that?"

"But you're not struggling," Crowe observed.

"I don't want to go overboard," Pearson explained, "also the police are coming."

Everyone looked at the port. Police boats charged towards them. Crowe put the boat in gear, and they sprang across the water. The police boats had a late start, but their vessels were built better than the Clinker. They would catch up in a matter of minutes.

Lost Miracle — 3:10 p.m.

Clinker and two police boats could be seen coming across the water. They were flies compared to the black ship waiting on the horizon. Power surged through Lost Miracle; it buzzed. A titan was coming alive. The box-like container on deck moved. It collapsed within itself, revealing a long-nosed cannon. The cannon rotated at its base. Power built up at the tip in the form of blue light.

The cannon maneuvered and aimed towards Boston. Buzzing noises continued to fill the air. A blue beam released from the barrel, sailing through the air, and hitting the Port of Boston. It disappeared once it made contact with the land. All the power was lost at the port. Everything within a mile of where the beam struck didn't have power anymore, including all vessels and vehicles.

The beam didn't affect the boats coming towards Lost Miracle, they were already too far out. But the black ship didn't waste time targeting the police with the cannon. A new buzzing sound came from underneath the water. Two different beams of light shot out from the old torpedo tubes the ship had. The beams shot underwater and hit their marks.

The police vessels lost all power. They would need someone to come out and tow them back to the dock. Giving the Clinker a chance to get away. The boat zoomed away from the port and continued to grow closer to Lost Miracle.

The black ship waited.

Lost Miracle will return in the next book in the series.

Next book will be called:

Lost Miracle Hallowed Sea

If you like Ann Riley's works, try reading "**Vital Era**".

Team Vital Era built the revolutionary Draconis Community. But can it be rescued, as it crumbles from within?

New Book Coming...

Also the next book to come out will be called "**Tied Souls**" (Jan 2019) and here is a little piece of the book.

Adam pulled out the closest chair for Tala before sitting down on the stool, not waiting for her to take the seat. Theo walked over to the other chair and sat down, while Tala seated herself.

"So how did Clare come to you?" Theo asked.

"My carriage stopped in the middle of town. And while I was out she... materialized. It truly shocked me, so I followed her all the way to a strange dense smoke surrounding Adam," Tala explained.

"I didn't see any smoke," Adam commented.

Theo ignored him, "Miss Solomon you may not realize it, but you saw a ghost."

Tala felt a little uneasy at his announcement, but she thought Clare was something strange.

"You, my dear, are a ghost dancer," he revealed, "like me."